A Night without Whispers

ALSO BY PIPER CJ

No Other Gods

The Deer and the Dragon

The Fox and the Falcon

The Night and Its Moon

The Night and Its Moon

The Sun and Its Shade

The Gloom Between Stars

The Dawn and Its Light

Accompanying *The Night and Its Moon* Novellas:

A Night Without Whispers

Wing and Arrow

A Year of Tea and Honey

Crown and Crumble

Villains

A Chill in the Flame

Fern's School for Wayward Fae

The Graveyard Gift

A Night without Whispers

odrin's story

PIPER CJ

To those of us who've cried over fictional characters—
We may be sad, but at least we have a book.

CONTENTS

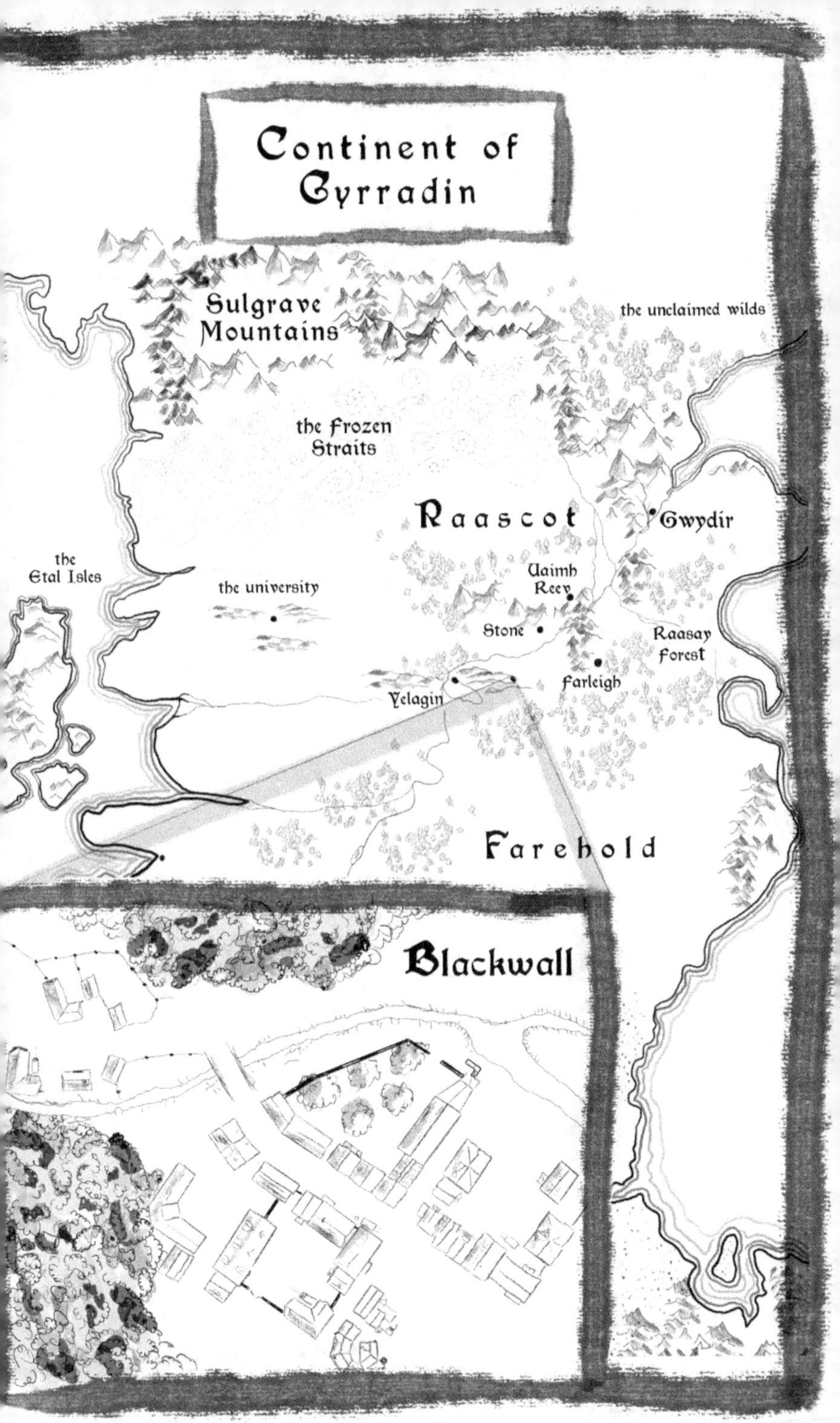

Continent of Gyrradin
Sulgrave Mountains
the unclaimed wilds
the Frozen Straits
Raascot
Gwydir
the Etal Isles
the university
Uaimh Reev
Stone
Raasay Forest
Farleigh
Yelagin
Farehold
Blackwall

PART ONE
FAWN

"Is it a bone?"

"It's from a deer. A boy deer."

"A buck?" She knew the word from hearing her father and his friends laugh around cuts of venison. She'd seen the unsightly horrors of game, pigs, and various other kills hung upside down to drip-dry in the shed behind their butcher shop before they were carved and turned into sausages and meats. None of the animals she'd seen had bones like this. It twisted, coming to unusual points, darkening into shades of black and gray at the tip. It was nothing like the clean-picked bones discarded from her father's shop.

"Yes, a boy buck. It goes on its head. I've seen them."

"Did he die?" she asked, thinking of the deer suspended in the shed behind the shop. She picked it up and turned it over in her hands, looking for evidence of blood or injury on the bone.

"No!" He smiled. "The boy bucks lose them! They lose them all the time. It's like hair, I think."

"I don't lose my hair all the time."

Odrin smiled and stretched out his hand. The butcher's daughter passed it to him, and he examined the antler. He ran his fingers along the little treasure they'd found, feeling the smooth, ivory parts and the rough, treelike base. "I think you should keep it, Effie. It's a good treasure."

Effie returned the smile, asserting, "We can share it."

"You can't share an antler."

"Just watch me. I'll share it," she said. She took it back from him and clutched it in her fingers. They returned to the idle exercise of looking out over the village from the top of the hill, enjoying the tiny purple and white flowers that poked through the tall grass. A breeze made the grass ripple like the waves of a great body of water, each blade bending and dancing with the pieces beside it. Effie's muddy-brown hair whipped in the wind just like the grass. It would be in snarls before they left, but that was nothing unusual. She closed her eyes and enjoyed the warming rays of the sun, the smell of new leaves, and the presence of her only friend.

There were other children in their village, but not many.

The village cobbler had a girl a few years older than she was, but a few years was all it took for a child to lose interest in climbing trees, looking for pretty rocks, and catching frogs near the river—the cobbler's daughter preferred playing with dolls and boys and sparkly things now. The innkeeper had six children, all boys, but the gaggle of sons seemed to exist in a world of their own. Effie'd had a brother as well once. He and Odrin had been the best of friends. The butcher's son and the leather-smith's son were always running off to snare rabbits and fight with sticks, pretending they were knights or mercenaries. Effie was invited along, which was atypical in some families, but not hers. Her brother had been deeply good, always inclusive, always kind. The boys would give her a stick and let her fight, they'd boost her up as they scrambled over rooftops, they'd murmur appreciatively when she picked crayfish out of the river, unafraid of their pincers.

When a blood sickness took her brother after months of withering, Odrin hadn't let her be alone.

The noon bell sounded from the village's church.

"Guess we'd better go back for lunch," Odrin said, pushing himself to his feet and wiping his hands on his pants.

Effie bent to pick a purple flower and extended it to him, frowning. "If I'm going home with the antler, you can go home with a flower."

He put it behind on top of his head. "Do I look like a boy buck?"

She giggled and picked a few more flowers, sticking them in his hair until he had white and purple antlers of his own. The high sound of a woman's voice called up the hill and over the wind. Effie's mother was summoning her for mealtime.

✦

"I have two presents," the young girl said, grinning conspiratorially as her hazel eyes sparkled.

"Is the first one bread?" Odrin asked.

He had smelled sourdough baking when he'd walked by her house earlier while on an errand for his father, and he'd almost knocked on the door, but his mom had taught him not to ask for things that weren't offered—it came across as begging, she'd said. Earlier that day at the shop, his father had used too much force and bent the tool required for punching holes in leather while crafting a rather intricate belt, and once the man's stream of obscenities had died down, he'd given Odrin five pennies and told him to run and ask to borrow a mallet from the carpenter. If Odrin hadn't been on an important mission, he would have stopped to see Effie. He didn't hate helping his father out in the shop, but he'd prefer swimming in the river and chasing her around with snakes as the serpents wiggled and she screamed.

"Close!" She shook her head at his guess. "It's sausage, for your father, though I guess it can be for you too."

He frowned. "Did my dad buy sausages?"

Procuring something from her pocket, she shrugged. "We traded. I promised him some of our sausages, so he'd help me with these."

"How did you do this!" Odrin gasped, his eyes widening as he turned the necklace over in his hand. A thin strap of doubled-up leather created a circle, with two tight knots that allowed him to adjust its size. The leather threaded through the antler's single tip, making the necklace look more like a tooth than part of a deer.

"I asked my dad to help cut them up and your dad to make the strap! One for you, and one for me." She put the antler-tip necklace over her head, tightening one of the knots so it hung just below the small dip between her collarbones. "Here, let me help you." Effie loosened the knot to get it over Odrin's head, then tightened it so it rested securely around his neck without being too tight. "Do you like it?"

"I love it." He smiled. He really did. It was better than bread.

"I told you I'd find a way to share!"

PART TWO
YEARLING

"If you don't stop hanging out with that girl into all hours of the night, you're going to get her pregnant." His mother frowned. "I raised you to be better than that."

Odrin had an apple in his mouth like a stuck pig, holding it with his teeth as he shrugged into a jacket. It was too late into autumn to get far without a coat, but he'd debated forgoing the jacket altogether. It was an issue of income rather than vanity that had him cringing whenever he caught his reflection. He disliked the way its cuffs ended just before the knobby points of his wrists. Odrin was almost too lanky for his clothes, and before long his mother would have to start letting them out or work an entirely new homespun wardrobe.

"I've told you, it's not like that with her."

His mother rolled her eyes, face glowing against the firelight from the hearth, exacerbating her disapproval with shadows. She glared and said, "It never is, until it is. You're not old enough to take a wife, but you are old enough to get us all in trouble. Stay in the shop with your father. He needs the help. You know his health—"

"He's done working for the night," Odrin said, waving her away. Jacket fully on, he bit into the apple. He pulled his socks and feet into his boots. "He finished an hour ago and left for the tavern."

Her eyes blazed at the information. She set down her knitting and balled her hands into her fists, grabbing the wool cloak that she kept by the door as she stormed out of the house without another word. He'd known it would get his father in trouble, and he hadn't truly cared. He knew enough of their finances to know that they hadn't been making enough for his father to be spending what little they made in the shop on ale. Ever since the cobbler had taken it upon himself to add leather-smithing to his list of skills, their family had suffered greatly. There was food on the table and they had shoes without holes, but it was nothing like the happy, comfortable childhood he'd had. He knew that was his mother's true worry. She couldn't be responsible for another mouth to feed.

Six houses, two tall oak trees, a vendor's stall, and one turned corner away lived the butcher's family. While the leathersmith's home had a roof that needed patching and gutters that failed them each spring, the butcher's home remained a beacon of the community.

Odrin ran a hand through his hair to smooth it back as he approached Effie's house. Rather than knock, he slipped around to the side. He reached into his pocket for a pebble, but before he had a chance to throw it at her window, he heard something over his shoulder.

"Looking for someone?"

He spun to observe her casual lean. Grinning, he asked, "Ready for trouble?"

"Always," she said, arms crossed over her chest. Her weight remained relaxed against the shed behind the shop. She pulled her hips, now curving with the signs of her teenage years, up and off the wall, leaning only her shoulders into the shop as she stared at him from her angled vantage point. She wasn't being particularly sneaky. He probably should have spotted her sooner, but he'd been focused.

"Trouble" was something they defined loosely. Their version of trouble was just as much escapism as it was profit. They'd stumbled upon the overgrown remnants of an orchard only four months prior, complete with a dilapidated, lichen-covered shack, an old stone well, and the splintered remains of a wooden wheelbarrow. At the time, the young, green apples were far too tart, even if the twisted trees and abandoned tools provided endless fascination. Now, the late-fall day urged them to hurry and pick the ripe apples before they fell to the forest floor and rotted. Tonight would be their fourth trip this week alone. At least six trees still bore fruit, and if they didn't hurry, the ruby-red apples would plop to the ground to be pecked at by birds and become one with the earth.

Two empty burlap sacks with thick shoulder straps rested near Effie's feet. She scooped them up, and she and Odrin set off into the evening toward their treasure trove. Ideally, they would have left in the morning and returned for supper, but she had to help cut and dice and grind the meat in her parents' shop just as Odrin was required to hammer and shape leather with his father. Their adventures in the orchard had to wait until the workday was done.

With the sausage made and the leather molded, it was time to seek their trouble.

Collecting apples in their secret place was fun. It gave them something to do. It also gave them sacks and sacks of apples to sell for ciders, pies, and tarts, and it certainly didn't hurt to keep produce in their family's cabinets. If it was anything like their countless other trips to the orchard, their evening would comprise an afternoon of plucking fruit, of sharing stories, and of eating candy-sweet apples until their stomachs ached.

It usually took them just shy of an hour to hike to the orchard, but they walked a little more slowly tonight. Something about the red and brown leaves, the autumnal decay that smelled like perfume, and the vibrant colors of the sky told them not to hurry. They chatted about the usual things. The cobbler's daughter and the innkeeper's oldest son were to be married. Odrin's mother was more than likely going to make his father sleep on the floor that night. Effie despised the smell of blood and never wanted to eat meat again. Odrin suspected that his mother was going to tan his hide if she caught him giving milk to the stray cat. Effie had gotten in trouble for wasting money by tossing coins into the fountain while making wishes. They hated going to church and planned to fake stomachaches whenever their parents attempted to force them to sit through services.

When he spoke with Effie, Odrin was afforded a luxury he couldn't get anywhere else in the world. It was the most precious gift two young minds could offer one another.

They let themselves dream.

They would dream of the heroes in stories, of the ocean, of the merfolk and dragons and their first sight of the city. They dreamed of leaving their village, kissing their parents on the cheek, and saying goodbye to their tiny town in the woods. They dreamed of wielding power and magic and soaring with the black-winged angels of Raascot. They dreamed of ships and fish and the fabled university. They'd just begun to approach the orchard as their dreams turned into an uncomfortable lull.

"What is it?" Effie asked, unshouldering her bag. She reached up for the first apple of the day.

Odrin didn't know how to say what he wanted to say. He'd never been good at speaking his mind. He wasn't proud of this quality, but he did his best to overcome his nerves. His fingers flexed and relaxed as he fought a roll of anxious nausea. Now or never, he thought, it was time to test the waters between them.

"It could be easy for you," he said carefully. "To move

away, that is. If you wanted to marry a traveler, you could go to the city. You could find adventure."

The autumnal trees trembled, even the smallest wind causing several brightly colored leaves to detach from the branches and dance lazily to the forest floor. Effie's back had been to him as he spoke. He stared nervously at her, watching her posture, the curve of her shoulders, the tilt of her head, awaiting a reaction. It almost felt like he was looking at an angel from a fairy story. The beautiful Effie, surrounded by magical rubies and oranges and evening light. A single apple thudded from a tree in the distance, yet another overly ripe fruit relinquishing its grip for the season.

Effie plucked her second apple. The ripe fruit didn't resist as it fell into her hands. Her lips twisted to the side as she turned to eye Odrin. He met Effie's gaze for a long, uncertain moment before averting his eyes. They went to his feet, shame filling him. Odrin was sixteen. He should be able to stand up for himself, to tell her how he felt, to be strong and intentional with his language. Instead, he was a coward. He didn't want to risk alienating her by sharing affections she might not return. He probably would have kept his eyes on his shoes if he hadn't caught the pale flicker of her hand as she extended her open palm toward him.

"Give it," she said.

"What?" he asked, looking up at her.

"Your necklace. Give it to me."

Odrin's heart dropped into his stomach.

"No!"

"Odrin—"

This was so much worse than rejection. A torrent of thoughts and emotions poured through him like competing waves of blood and water. One flooded his ears with the pain of knowing he never should have said anything, scolding him for prying. The other drowned him in the regret of knowing he shouldn't have wanted anything from her other than friendship.

His hand flew to where the piece of antler hid beneath his shirt.

"I'm sorry, Eff. I didn't mean—"

"Give it to me," she said a little more firmly, wiggling her fingers for emphasis.

His face turned an unbecoming shade of gray-green. Odrin had daydreamed of so many things, good and bad. He'd imagined marrying Effie in the happiest of dreams. In waking nightmares, he foresaw a future where she left, where she moved on, where she found a better life. One thing he hadn't imagined was a path where she took back the very token that had united them for eight years.

His lips parted, his mouth drying as if it had been a year since his last drink. The waters within him did nothing for the terrified thirst for forgiveness that gripped him now. His fingers remained wrapped tightly around his pendant, clutching it to his chest. Seconds stretched into years before it became clear that she would not drop her hand. Odrin began to tug at the knot from the necklace, feeling the very threads of his heart unravel with it. In nearly a decade, he'd never removed it, so it required a bit of finessing to loosen. He began to pull it over his head, feeling a dizzying bloodlessness overtake him.

"Effie, I'm sorry. I didn't mean—"

She rolled her eyes and snatched it from him, plopping herself firmly to the forest floor amidst the overripe apples that had already fallen and begun to decay. He stared at the top of her light-brown hair, always a little wavy, a little snarled, a little unkempt, as she didn't bother with fancy combs or braids or careful preening. Effie dug in her pocket and found the small pocketknife she always had on her. She squinted, eyeing the antler. She bit her lip as she focused, carving three parallel lines and one vertical line into the tip. When she finished, she abandoned the piece in her lap as she loosened her own knot and restarted the process.

The tumultuous storm of Odrin's pain had lessened, its raindrops calming into the gentle pitter-patter of confusion.

"What are you doing?"

"Give me a minute."

"Eff—"

"Damn it, why couldn't your name have begun with the letter i? Do you know how hard it is to carve an o? Is a square close enough to a circle?"

Just like that, the cut threads of his heart begin to sew themselves together. He gaped at her where she sat on the ground and slowly lowered himself to sit beside her. His fingers flexed against his knees as if struggling to contain his energy. Odrin tried to catch her gaze, but she was too focused on her task, face twisted in concentration as her fingers worked.

"You're carving our initials?"

"Well, I'm trying, but *o* is such a goddess-damned-hard… There! That should do it," she panted proudly, as if carving had been quite the exhausting task. She remained cross-legged on the ground, offering him a broad smile. "Here. You keep the e, and I'll keep the o, how's that sound?"

She was finished. With a rather unceremonious yank, Effie slipped the necklace with Odrin's initial around her head, scooping her hair to the side so it could rest gently beneath her locks. The antler dangled near her sternum. She then lifted the remaining pendant and carefully draped it over Odrin. She leaned in close to help him tighten the strap, her face only a few inches from his.

Her fingers stilled, softening slightly as they relaxed against the tender place where his shoulder met his neck.

Whether it was the smell of the apples, the magical spell that always seemed to accompany the colors of sunset, or the sheer relief at realizing that something he'd been so sure was set to be rejected turned out to be something entirely wonderful, he didn't know, but he felt years of cautious desire bubble within him. He swallowed against the knot in his throat, but it felt as though he'd tried to consume an entire egg, shell and all. The knot remained as he leaned in ever so slightly.

She didn't pull her hands away. One remained on the space just shy of his neck, while the other gently pressed into his chest. Her large, hazel eyes swirled with speckles of greens, browns, and golds as rich as the forest around her as she met his deep, earthy gaze. He was terrified, but he didn't look away. He didn't know much of love, or of women, but he knew Effie, and he knew with every stitch in his body that he wanted to kiss her. She didn't move away, staying inches from his face as they sat on the orchard floor, and, if only for a heartbeat, he thought that she might want to kiss him too.

A snap broke the fragile thing between them, tension fracturing as she turned her head toward the noise.

"What was that?"

"Probably a rabbit?" he offered, hoping they could salvage the moment.

"No, listen." She strained her ears. He listened, and he heard it too.

Breathing.

Worry began to mix with whatever emotion he'd felt only seconds before. Were there wolves in the forest? What could he possibly do if a wolf had come upon them? He looked to Effie, then back to the trees, desperately searching his mind for how he might protect her from a wolf.

Heavy, loud breathing echoed steadily through the forest. There was a rattling quality to the inhalations and exhalations that Odrin had never heard before, as if each breath was a gust of wind dragged over loose nails in tin cans. What could be so large that they could hear its chuffing from where they sat?

"Give me your knife," he said quietly.

"Get your own knife," she whispered back. She wrapped her fingers tightly around the small hilt. It was barely sufficient to peel a vegetable, let alone do her any real good if they should need it.

He slowly began to rise to his feet, straining his eyes against the rapidly fading light. Odrin extended his arm for a fallen tree branch. His fingers wrapped around the rough bark of the large stick, lifting it to his side. He'd played knight using sticks in the forest for years as a child. It may just have to suffice now.

A second, louder noise crashed through the forest. This was not the subtle snaps of twigs or the prowling of beasts but the thundering sounds of hooves, the breaking of branches, the clanging of metal, the cracking and bursting and breaking of the forest around them as something sprinted right toward them. Odrin yanked Effie to her feet and shoved her behind him moments before an enormous black shape lunged from the shadows.

Fear burned hotter than fire and colder than frostbite as every limb filled with terror.

Effie screamed as teeth, claws, eyes, and black, amphibious skin glinted against the dying light. The monster snarled a horrible, otherworldly growl as it snapped at them. They scarcely had time to take a single step back to remove themselves from its path. The creature nearly knocked them to the ground as it careened beyond them, gracelessly crashing into the dilapidated shack. Perhaps it had meant to push off the structure in order to turn and leap into the forest at an angle, but the aged wood had crumbled beneath it, thwarting its escape.

A second, earthshaking sound made itself known. With a loud battle cry, a man on a horse broke through the forest. He dismounted and shouted for Odrin and Effie to get away. He barely looked in their direction as he took off toward the part-canine, part-feline monstrosity. Odrin's fingers dug into Effie's arm as the two remained frozen in shock.

"Go!" the stranger yelled, fury and urgency pouring out of the command.

The armed man prepared himself to battle the beast, sword out and ready. Odrin's slack-jawed stare darted from the warrior to where the monstrous canine was still pulling itself from the splinters of the shack. The demon shook the impact from its body and turned, knobby spine poking up through its back as it focused its glinting eyes on the stranger. He cried out toward the monster, antagonizing it, urging it to make the first move.

Odrin and Effie couldn't stay, but the boy's jelly legs had forgotten how to flee. He shoved Effie farther and farther back as they stumbled away from the creature.

"Let's go!" she shouted, pulling on his sleeve. She forced him to run. Once his feet got going, they didn't stop.

The pair skidded past the stranger's horse and twisted through the trees, running toward the village. They slashed at low-hanging branches and scrambled through patches of this-tles. Somewhere behind them, the beast's murderous cries echoed through the forest moments before the wet, crunching sound of steel and flesh joined the cacophony of noises. They stumbled over roots and bounded through crunchy, fallen leaves. Their lungs burned as much as their arms and legs, their panting just one of the many noises in the chaotic forest.

They were running so fast they almost didn't see it before it was too late.

Vageth.

Odrin knew the word. He'd heard the stories. He'd seen the drawings.

The houndlike creature was poised in a tree blocking their path, ready to leap down like a mountain cat. It spread its blackened mouth as if to smile, though surely these creatures held no emotion, only hunger. Saliva dripped from his open maw, running over thousands of needlelike teeth as it eyed the teenagers. Its talons flexed on the large bough as it tensed to pounce.

"Go back to the man!" Odrin commanded Effie.

"I'm not going to—"

Before she had a chance to argue, the vageth dove from the tree and bounded toward Odrin. He lifted the stick above his head as Effie turned and ran toward the stranger. He could hear her screaming for the man to help them, but he was too focused on the creature's snarls to hear if her cries were answered. At least she would be safe.

The vageth lunged, and by little more than sheer dumb luck, Odrin swung with enough force to knock it out of its path for his jugular. He readied himself to swing again just as the whir of one arrow, then another, sliced the air and embedded themselves between the animal's ribs. Rather than fall, as would any normal beast, it turned its terrible attention toward the archer.

The stranger ran for it, dropping his bow and lifting his sword once more.

The arc of his blade had been too fast for Odrin to see. He scarcely caught the high, ringing sound of steel and a glint of silver. The fight was over before it had begun.

The forest no longer smelled of apples and autumn and the hope of teenage love. Waves of sulfur and carrion bubbled up from the tarlike substance that oozed from the dog's decapitated remains. The stranger lifted his sword, slicing the fallen creature again and again until it was in a few different parts. He wiped his forehead with his sleeve and looked at Odrin.

"Thank you." Odrin could barely speak. He didn't know what to say. He scarcely knew what had happened.

"Neither of you has any cuts? No wounds?" the man asked, voice like thunder. He stared at them seriously, armed to the gills with more blades and weaponry than Odrin had ever seen.

Odrin shook his head.

"Good, because if this demon's blood gets in your system, your infection will never heal. Go get my shovel from my horse, boy. Show your gratitude by helping me separate and bury the pieces."

Small, light, tentative footsteps joined the sounds of their shovels through the earth as Effie rejoined them.

"Who are you?" she asked, eyes still wide.

Odrin looked between them, eyeing the way her gaze was a mixture of shock, gratitude, and admiration while she stared at the assassin.

The man sighed, finishing up his shallow grave. He looked at her from where he knelt on the ground, tar covering his hands and knees, fresh earth pressed before him.

"I'm a reever."

Effie–

> *I'm a coward, and I always have been.*
>
> *I was too afraid to tell you that you were the kindest, bravest, most wonderful person in the world, too afraid to tell you that I didn't want other friends, anyone else to catch frogs with or climb the hill behind the village or play knights and swords with, too afraid to tell you that I wanted you to run away with me, too afraid to kiss you in the orchard, too afraid to save you when you needed me.*
>
> *I don't want to be a coward anymore.*
>
> *My parents don't need the extra mouth to feed, and you don't need a man who can't protect you, who can't speak his mind, who can't live in truth.*
>
> *I've left for the mountains. I don't know much of reevers, but I know that even if I arrive a coward, I'll become someone worthy, or I'll die trying.*

Marry. See the world. Be happy. Live a full, wonderful life.

My happiness will be in seeing your happiness.

Someday I'll be able to protect you, your guardian angel, a man who might have been worthy of you.

My heart will belong to no one else.

—Odrin

PART THREE
HIDE

Time passed, as it does.

Moments became days became months became years. Legs grew, muscles filled, early signs of age stubbled on the chin or wrinkled in the corner of eyes. Skills and lessons and people filtered in and out of his life, just as pain came and went. Winters melted, summers faded, every autumn came with apples, though none tasted as sweet as the ripened fruit that might have been plucked from the fingers of the one he loved.

One moment he'd had his whole life ahead of him, and the next he'd either be satisfied that he'd lived it to its fullest or realize he'd wasted his time on the earth with the foolish belief that he had more time.

PART FOUR
RUTTING

He shouldn't be so afraid to return. He'd spent years in Uaimh Reev learning to conquer his fear, hadn't he? But passing through his village on this dispatch brought up a wellspring of emotions he wasn't sure he was ready to face. He didn't know if his parents would be happy to see him or if they'd curse him for leaving when they'd needed him to take over the shop and continue the family business. He had no idea if it would hurt him or help him to walk by old vendors, to get supplies from the innkeeper, or to hear the nostalgia of the church's noon bell. Mostly, he wasn't sure that he could handle seeing Effie with her husband and collection of beautiful, wonderful children—if she'd stayed at all.

What would be worse? To enter the village and find she'd moved to the sea to become a ship captain's wife? To pass by the butcher's shop only to find it empty? Or to see her face in the toddlers and younglings who ran around the village, half her, and half whatever man had won her heart?

He couldn't stay on the hilltop overlooking the village forever. No, even the hill itself brought him a nostalgia akin to sorrow. Its grasses still bent and swayed in the breeze just like a lake, a river, an ocean as they mixed with the purple and white flowers he had once worn in his hair as a buck. Perhaps he cast quite the striking silhouette—a man on his horse against the lavenders of morning light overlooking the village —but ten years was long enough to wait. Either he returned now, or not at all. If he hadn't run out of provisions the day before, he may have opted for the latter. Instead, he clicked his tongue and urged his horse down the hill and into his hometown.

Now or never.

Odrin tethered his horse outside of his parents' home and knocked at the door. He waited for a beat before lowering his hand to twist the knob. To his surprise, it was not his mother's face that peered back at him when it opened.

Effie's mouth dropped, her lips parted in a silent gasp. The glass pitcher she'd been holding tumbled from her hands, shattering to the floor into shards with her surprise. She inhaled sharply, then immediately knelt, shaking her head as if rejecting the possibility of his presence. Her unbound, muddy-brown hair tumbled around her face in waves, covering her shoulders.

"Oh my goddess, Effie." His words came out rushed and breathless as he bent and began to help her gather the pieces of glass just as she gasped in pain. A particularly jagged shard sliced into her palm, red blood already flowing freely over onto the floor. She was still too stunned to truly react, to look at him, to address the impossibility at the door. "Come on," he urged as he pushed her inside his parents' home and to the kitchen. He grabbed a rag to stop the bleeding.

Breaths still coming out in soft, shallow gasps, she took a while to speak.

"I never thought I'd see you again," she said, hazel eyes wide with disbelief. Dark purple bruises smudged beneath her eyes. She was still so young, barely in her midtwenties, but her wind-chafed skin showed years of stress.

Odrin didn't know where to start. He didn't know how to feel, how to act, or what to ask. He said the first thing that came to mind, even if he didn't care for the answer nearly as much as he did about her presence.

He looked around. "Where are my parents?"

She looked to her palm as blood began to blot through the rag, staring at it sadly where it rested between his two large, calloused hands. Maybe the red helped her shock begin to subside, maybe the painful reality of the injury helped her to gather her bearings, but after an awfully long pause, she answered him.

"Your father passed away years ago, Odrin. I'm so sorry. Your mother—"

"What about my mother?"

She swallowed. "She's not been well. With no one to take care of her, I…"

"Does she live?"

His heart squeezed with pain and hope and confusion as he looked at the hand in his own. She wore no ring. She hadn't journeyed to the coast, or lived a life of adventure, or married. She'd moved in with his mother as her caretaker. He was so overcome he felt as though his lungs had been shredded, left bloodied and useless within his chest. For a moment, he imagined this was how it would feel to drown on dry land.

Effie nodded, still not looking at him. Her tone, her distant voice, the slump of her shoulders told a clear message. She thought him little more than a phantom. She couldn't look him in the eye.

"She's asleep," Effie said finally. "She spends most of her days and nights asleep upstairs in her room. I know she'll be happy to see you." Her gaze remained on the cloth as crimson continued to saturate the fabric.

"Goddess, this cut is deep. Hold on."

He disappeared out the front door and reappeared with a small, brown glass bottle from his saddlebags. Odrin dribbled a bit into her hand and told her to drink what remained of the tonic while he set to work sweeping up the remnants of the pitcher. Once the house was clean, he sat with Effie and listened to her talk quietly and slowly of the last decade. She told him of the village, of their families, of how she'd cried for weeks when she'd found his letter. She told him she'd made it as far as Stone the year he left, intent on chasing him down only six months after he'd abandoned her. Once she'd reached the town at the edge of the kingdom and looked up at the mountain, she'd realized that he'd left his life behind to find a new one altogether. She couldn't bring herself to tear him from his destiny.

She'd stayed at the inn in Stone for three nights, staring at the mountain every day, listening to the townsfolk speak reverently of their league of guardians before eventually she'd left, knowing he would not return.

She'd accepted it, and yet, she hadn't.

They exchanged stories as the hours stretched on.

He told her of his years of training, of his many bruises, and cuts, and the time he'd nearly tripped down a cliff. He told her about his dispatches, the demons, the studies, the tonics, and his oath. He spoke of the twenty men who lived in Uaimh Reev and their lives, their personalities, even his knowledge and work with the fae. She'd never met a member of the fae but watched him recount his stories with a far-off look as if he were telling fairy tales.

"And now?" she asked quietly. "You're on dispatch again?"

He looked at her for a long time, then raised a hand to brush her cheek.

"I am," he said.

She closed her eyes as if the contact brought her pain. It looked as though she was trying not to cry. "And when you finish your dispatch? You'll return to the reev?"

He left his hand against her cheek and softly responded, "I'll be a reever no matter where I live. Effie, if you'll have me, I'd like it to be here."

She opened her eyes, looking up at him as if studying his face for signs of a cruel joke. He could see the way her breath caught in her throat, anxiety, hope, and hurt all visible and audible as the emotions colored both her face and the very air that left her lungs.

With his free hand, he tugged at the collar of his tunic to reveal a small antler pendant engraved with a single letter. She nearly choked on her laugh, her uninjured hand flying to cover her mouth. Effie stood and reached her arms around him to hug him, but before she realized what was happening, he'd joined her on her feet. What had been intended as an embrace became the kiss they'd never shared. She felt so tiny against his towering shape, but he cradled her with a gentleness and a tenderness that promised to wash away the pain of her hard life. He cupped the back of her head, pressed his hand against her lower back, and enveloped her in a promise to never let go.

The kiss tasted like seawater, so wet from the tears she'd spent more than ten years withholding. When she'd returned from Stone, she'd vowed to be strong, just as he'd left to become resilient, brave, and worthy. Maybe she didn't need to be strong anymore.

His old room—the one downstairs—had been where she'd stayed for her years in the home. It would be their room now.

Their kiss was more than a kiss.

It was relief, it was need, it was gratitude and longing and remorse for the years they'd lost. Her dress slipped easily off her shoulders. He reached into the center of his shirt and pulled it up over his head from the back, revealing not the boy she'd known but a man with a hardened chest, ready for battle. Though he looked like the young warrior of ballads, he touched her, held her, kissed her, tasted her, cared for her with more gentleness than she could fathom. He took his time with her, stretching their day into moments that lasted an eternity, every heartbeat, every breath, every caress and stroke and kiss a delicate, perfect thing that couldn't be hurried. It was more beautiful than poetry or flowers or songs or jewels or sunsets or the first thunderstorm in spring. It was a moment that artists only wished they'd captured when they painted, a purity that bards longed to bottle in their music, a day that writers and lovers around the world would have traded their lives for, for a single taste. When they finished making love, she cried once more in his arms. Her cheek rested against his chest, soaking in the steady sound of his heart as it beat only for her.

He kissed the top of her head, pulling her against his chest.

"Don't cry, Eff," he said quietly. "Don't cry. All I wanted was for you to be happy."

She sniffed. "You are my happiness."

✦

He'd loved every dispatch—before this, of course.

He enjoyed the thrill of the fight, the satisfaction of victory, and the justice of vanquishing evil in their endless pursuit for magical balance. This would be the first dispatch he despised and, if he was lucky, his last dispatch for a long, long time. He hadn't wanted to tear himself away from her. He'd stayed three days longer than he was supposed to, greeting his mother, though she scarcely knew he was there, and holding his beloved. Effie couldn't so much as peel a potato without Odrin standing behind her, arms wrapped around her, nuzzling into her neck.

"The sooner you go, the sooner you can come back," she'd murmured.

"I will be back this time."

She'd adjusted her grip on the potato peeler and turned to him, hazel eyes too lovely to be truly stern. She glared. "Odrin, goddess help you if you do not return. You had your one chance to escape me, and you blew it. We're together now."

His heart had tightened and swelled all at once.

They were together now.

He'd need to try to clear his head if he was to focus and stay alive long enough to finish his dispatch. Rumors and ravens had been filtering to Uaimh Reev over a merchant who'd been suspected of keeping a sustron to swindle others and amass his wealth. Sustrons' blood could be used to conceal and camouflage, meaning that if the rumors were true, it was quite likely that the merchant had not earned a penny of his money honestly. Sustrons were a twofold threat, both for their bloodthirst and for the unfair advantage they offered their keeper. If the merchant truly had one, not only was he operating as the city's phantom, but if his creature got loose, he'd be responsible for the piles of corpses from the first bloodsucker the city had seen in a century.

It had taken four days of hard riding to reach the city but only moments of inquiry regarding the merchant for everyone in town to point Odrin in the right direction. From the quake of their fingers and the rage in their eyes, they may have hoped he had arrived to assassinate the merchant himself. Clearly, the sustron's owner was not particularly well liked. One vendor had even begged to escort Odrin to the estate, eager to watch the events unfold, but Odrin had waved him away. If he was going to sneak up on a man and his sustron, he couldn't afford the attention of an audience.

Even from the outside, the estate itself looked like any in Farehold—gaudy, wasteful, and like a monument to overcompensation. Odrin forewent the front door to sneak around back, looking for the servants' entrance. It had been a good idea in theory, but the moment he rounded the corner and nearly caused a woman to scream out in fright, he regretted his choice.

He was between the shadows of the coniferous bushes, and

with his weapons and hardened, leather armor, he doubtlessly struck an intimidating silhouette.

"Shh," he urged her, flattening his palms to show he meant no harm.

She raised her hands as well, taking a fearful step backward. She was pale and sickly-looking, not from the fright he'd given her but as if the gauntness of stress and starvation had whittled away at her flesh and muscles until little remained. This woman did not live a good life.

"Please, sir, don't hurt us."

He shook his head. "I'm not here to hurt any person."

Odrin studied her as the last word soaked in. The emotion on her face changed as she understood his meaning. She lowered her voice to match his whisper.

"You're here to slay the demon?"

He inhaled through the nose, grateful for her confirmation. He nodded. "What do you know of it? Where does he keep it?"

Her eyes darted toward the door, anxious that she might be caught.

"It's evil."

"Where?" he pressed, taking a step closer, revealing himself fully from the juniper bushes.

"The root cellar." She kept her voice low, strangled with worry. "There's a latch in the kitchen hidden under the rug. I can get you in, but you have to wait until the master of the house goes to sleep."

This might not be such a terrible dispatch, after all. He'd been sent to investigate and kill a demon, and clearly no one in the city, nor under his own roof, had any love for the man or his captive beast. Odrin agreed, and she gestured to the toolshed, promising she'd return to fetch him in a few hours. The toolshed wasn't his favorite place to be. It wasn't terribly dignified to wait amidst the spades, rakes, and burlap sacks of manure, but he knew how to be patient. Hours passed, but they felt like no time at all. He calmed himself, knowing the sooner he killed the sustron, the sooner he could return home so Effie could make an honest man out of him. It was all he wanted, and that longing was strong enough to replace the smell of manure and earth with the memories tinged with ripe apples and autumn days.

The woman was true to her word. He wasn't sure what she knew of sustrons, but if the estate's attendants knew the demon would puncture their throats and drain them until they were little more than husks if it broke free, their reasons for wanting it dead were all too understandable.

"Will you be loud?" she whispered, pausing before opening the door to the estate.

"The creature will scream."

"Will you kill the master as well?"

He shook his head, which seemed to disappoint her.

"I'm sorry," he said. "I'm only here to restore balance. A captive demon is anything but. I cannot kill your master unless he turns a hand to me." He watched her expression and then amended, "I see the thought behind your eyes and will ask you only once not to wake him in the hope that he confronts me. I'm a reever. I'm not here as an assassin. I'm here to kill the demon infesting your home."

She swallowed, clearly ashamed that her thought had been so transparent. Perhaps for tonight, murdering the blood-sucking demon would be feat enough.

"Leave the hatch to the root cellar open. I'll kill the sustron and be out of your estate before the master has a chance to put his feet in his slippers. I'll leave the property with its head and bury it apart from the body, but you'll want to have some of the other servants help you bury the torso. Can you do that? If you work quickly, it could be gone by the time the master comes downstairs, and then he'll think the creature escaped rather than was killed."

She nodded, understanding his plan.

"Right. Then he won't know we helped someone find it. He won't suspect us."

"Precisely. Have you seen it? Do you know how it's held?"

She shivered at the memory. "There's an iron manacle around its neck, chained to the wall. A big, thick one."

He cursed under his breath but wasn't surprised. Unfortunately, he would not be able to behead it as he'd hoped if a thick metal shackle remained between its chin and shoulders. If he swung for the torso, the upper body would remain intact, alive, including its monstrous head. He'd have to hack through the skull. The bisection would be neither clean nor quick.

The moment they entered the home, he was hit with the horrible stench of cologne. It was as if every thread of fabric in the house had been soaked in the man's perfume. Odrin's eyes watered against the overwhelming smell. Perhaps this was an effort to conceal the sulfuric odors of the merchant's demon, but Odrin would rather smell spoiled eggs than choke through the thick cloud of musk and sandalwood.

He hated everything about the home, inside and out.

From the stuffy, gilded, flowery displays of wealth that clung to every inch of the walls to the tables, shelves, armoires, furniture, chandeliers, and even the gold-plaited crown molding on the ceiling, there wasn't an inch of the estate he didn't find revolting.

He kept his displeasure to himself as the servant led him quietly into the kitchen. She pulled back the rug, and just as she had said, there was a hatch to a root cellar. She took a deep breath for bravery before lifting the covering and allowing a ladder to unfold down into the pit of darkness.

A new stench wafted up from the cellar—not just the smell of the monster but the putrid odor of rancid blood and decay.

He'd been hardened against most things, but it took all his training not to gag.

"I'll get you a candle, sir," she whispered. She was gone

then and at his side again in a flash. She handed him a lit candle with a trembling hand.

"Ready the other servants," he said. "Be prepared to carry the demon out."

She nodded in confirmation before taking off for the servants' quarters.

Odrin lowered himself into the basement, drowning in the dizzying odor of death. The flame was small, but in the dark cellar, it immediately illuminated everything he needed to see. Countless bodies—mostly animal, though some bones appearing suspiciously human—littered the floor. Then he saw the reason he'd come. Against the far wall, the sustron snapped to attention, instantly hissing as he entered. It crouched, hugging the wall for a moment as its black eyes widened.

Odrin set the candle on the ground. "Let's get this over with."

Sustrons were the All Mother's sickest creation, he was sure of it. The black-and-white demon was nearly a praying mantis, its knees and elbows bending at improper angles, razor-sharp hands doubling back on the forearms. The torso was human-adjacent, its chest and midsection resembling something that could have been man or fae. The head atop its shoulders was nearly human as well, though unnaturally elongated. It opened its maw, dropping its jaw lower and lower as its black-tongued mouth extended nearly to its sternum, ready to plunge its twin fangs into the flesh of anything that dared approach. Odrin knew sustrons had one purpose. They'd been created to suck you dry and eat you whole.

The beast lunged for him but was yanked immediately backward by its manacle.

Though vile and fatal, they were not the most intelligent demons.

The sustron loosed an ear-splitting screech in protest. The moment it lost its footing, Odrin sprung for the advantage. He gripped the hilt of his sword with two hands, using all his power to puncture the creature's skull. He couldn't truly behead it, not with its neck protected, but if he cut close enough to the shackle, he might be able to slip the rest of the neck out through the chain once it was sliced. His sword met the crunch of bone, and the sustron screamed, the high, horrible sounds of agony, hunger, and hate.

It continued to writhe, its horrid, long, open mouth reaching for him as if it were yet another arm surrounded by spikes. The creature thrashed its mantislike talons, but Odrin remained just out of reach.

He grunted loudly as he brought his blade down again and again, cleaving in exactly the same place. It was enough. The top three quarters of the monstrous head skidded across the room, joining the carrion in its den of fallen prey. The creature fell, oil-like blood immediately pooling around it while its razor-sharp, insectlike arms continued to thrash.

"Fuck," he groaned, hoping it wouldn't come to this.

He chopped off one arm, then the next. Hopefully, chopping it to bits would make it easier for the servants to carry. With a grunt he shoved his boot into its humanoid torso to pin its chest against the wall and flipped his sword, shoving its hilt into the stump where the jaw and neck connected to the manacle, using sheer blunt force to push what was left of the demon downward through the shackle. It popped free, tumbling from the shackle as Odrin's effort was successful.

Black blood continued to spurt from the animated corpse, much of it soaking into the surrounding furs and rotting corpses of its discarded meals.

It was no surprise that the sustron had woken the house.

"Goddess damn it." He had to move quickly.

He heard several angry cries from upstairs and knew that there would be no escaping undetected. He sheathed his blade, leaving it sticky and filthy for the moment, as time was of the essence. He grabbed the piece of the skull that contained the top of its jaw and the fangs and tucked it under his arm, then reached for one of its insectlike arms before running for the ladder. Taking three rungs at a time and only able to use his free hand, he ran up the ladder to escape the estate.

He'd barely made it to the door when he realized something.

In a few moments, the merchant would descend the stairs to see his prize beast slain. There would be no way to convince the man that the sustron had merely escaped. If Odrin took off now, the master would doubtlessly blame his servants.

"Shit," he grumbled in anger, hating his conscience. He pinched his mouth as he did the only decent thing he could think to do. He needed to wait at the back door long enough for the merchant to see him. The man needed to know it was a stranger—an assassin, a mercenary, a rogue, a reever—and not blame the attendants who worked beneath him. Odrin cursed every single fucking second that passed between the minute it took the master of the house to reach the bottom of the stairs in his stupid, frilly, silky sleeping robes. The moment their eyes met, Odrin had done his job.

He kicked open the door and it swung outward, allowing him to spring for his horse. He'd barely had time to swing up into the saddle, merchant screaming after him, before he took off for the road. The angry stream of threats and obscenities faded away as his steed carried him toward the dark line where the sky met the earth. As soon as he could, he'd leave the road for the woods, bury his pieces of the demon, and return home.

Home.

The horse's thundering hooves as he galloped out of the city were the only noise in his ears. The moment they broke free from the city limits, he slowed his horse so as not to exhaust it. Fresh air finally replaced the horrible combination of death and cologne.

The pieces of sustron looked up at him, eyes still animated with its hatred.

"Don't I know it," Odrin agreed at the undead demon's wild, still-moving eyes. "Life never turns out quite the way we think it will, does it?"

◆

The way Effie cried when he returned made it clear that she had not truly believed she would see him again. Filthy from the road, stained with tarlike blood, and stinking of sulfur, Odrin swept her into his arms and spun her in a circle. His heart was so full. No dispatch or demon or force of nature could take this from him.

He was home.

PART FIVE
STAG

"You always choose the worst time of year to make your check-ins! Samael can wait. The reev isn't going anywhere. Don't go in the winter."

Odrin smiled through his spoonful of potatoes and root vegetables. Effie was an excellent cook, which was often challenging to accomplish in the coldest months of the year. Despite the lack of greens and fresh things available after Yule, she knew her way around a kitchen. She wasn't afraid of salt, bacon, or spice. Since Effie's father was the butcher, they never had to worry about going without meat.

"It's not winter! The ground has thawed, there's barely any snow clinging to the shady areas, and the days are much longer and warmer. Last year I also visited Uaimh Reev in the spring."

"You only went in spring last year because you went in the middle of the winter solstice the year prior, you masochist. And it was barely spring. A blizzard came upon you before you'd made it down the mountain! I swear, Odrin, you're going to be the death of me if you keep making me worry. You're trying to get yourself killed."

He shoveled in the rest of his food.

The gentle cooing from a bassinet in the corner let him know Yrsa was awake. His heart squeezed at the sound. It was his second favorite noise in the world, after his wife's laughter.

Effie had fought him on the name, but Odrin loved the idea of calling his little girl "she-bear." He was going to raise Yrsa to be as brave and strong as her parents, he swore. Eventually Effie had conceded, appreciating not only its meaning but the knowledge that her daughter would grow up able to fend for herself in the world. A woman should have her wits about her to simply stay alive, but it didn't hurt to have a few other tricks up her sleeve. They wanted to give Yrsa her best chance at life.

The days may have been getting longer, but dinnertime was still something that happened after dark. The glass windows reflected the black, moonless sky. The only light was the warm, popping fire that filled the home.

"I'll get her." Effie attempted to rise from her chair.

"No," he said as he shushed her, leaning across the table and planting a kiss on her cheek, "let me do it. I want to spend as much time with her as possible before I leave."

"Stop talking like you're riding off to your death! You already left me once for ten years."

"And I'll never live it down."

"You don't deserve to live it down." She rolled her eyes. She'd forgiven him long ago, but it did make it easy for her to win her arguments. He let her have it. He'd never leave again, and that unwavering loyalty was the only thing he could offer her in penance from now until his final breath. He crossed the room to where the bassinet sat near the fire keeping Yrsa warm, and he cradled her into his arms.

Effie rested her elbow on the table, making a fist and propping up her cheek with the gesture as she watched them.

"She looks just like your mother, don't you think?"

"Not at all." He shook his head, peering down at the perfect, tiny creation in his arms. "She looks like her mother. The most beautiful girl in the world."

He played with Yrsa, making faces as she babbled and giggled in his arms and as Effie bustled around the kitchen. He loved when she put her fat, tiny fingers against his mouth. He'd pretend to gobble them up, and she'd squeal in delight. His little she-bear wasn't quite a year old, and still too small to understand much, but she knew she loved her father and that her father loved her in return.

Dinner was wonderful. The evening was warm. The baby slept happily in her crib. The house was safe. The pantry was stocked. The one he loved was in his arms, in his bed. He drank her in, worshiping her between the sheets, holding her, filling her with everything he possessed from his body to his soul, cradling her as his wife wore nothing but the small, leather necklace that never left her throat—more sacred than rings, more valuable than diamonds. The symbol of their eternal connection.

This—their time in bed—was their church. She was his religion. He believed in their love the way bishops believed in the All Mother. If Odrin was pressed for his belief, he'd swear on the books that Effie was the goddess.

Still, at least once a year, he checked in on the reev and received dispatch. He wanted to make the world safer, not just for the good of the continent but the only two people he loved.

Gray dawn light filtered in through the window as his eyes fluttered open. He'd intended to wake before her, but he stirred from his sleep with her mouth working its way from his chest to someplace far more sensitive. He knew this trick, and it would most certainly work. She didn't want him to leave at first light, and he wouldn't. He'd never go to the reev again if she asked. He'd forsake the reevers forever if she so much as hinted that it was what she wanted. He'd stay in bed all morning. He'd stay in bed forever.

He gasped out against the pleasure of the wet, holy contact when her mouth found his manhood, but their bliss was cut short.

He would slaughter kings for his daughter, but goddess, if she didn't have terrible timing.

Effie poked her head up from beneath the sheets, brown hair askew.

"I'll get her."

He looked down and agreed that yes, maybe she should get the baby while he took a moment to compose himself and get dressed. Perhaps it wouldn't be the morning of lovemaking he'd hoped, but there would always be time. He drank tea with her by the fire, ensured they had two weeks of firewood already chopped, triple-checked the food, the healing tonics, the bandages, and made Effie repeat back to him everything he'd taught her about how to use a knife.

"You worry too much." She clucked her tongue.

He kissed Yrsa on the nose. "I'll be back, little one." Then to his wife, he offered his mouth, his hand on her cheek once more. "I'll be back," he said with low solemnity.

She kissed him back. "Go be the continent's guardian angel."

He shook his head. "I'm yours before anyone else's."

His favorite sight in the world, and it was too late in the day for him to truly appreciate it. It was a shame. He loved cresting the hill to see the shape of his village after a long trip away. It had been a particularly pleasant visit to the keep, with spirits high, men healthy, and no pressing dispatch required—though Samael had said he'd send a raven, should it be necessary. Odrin hoped he wouldn't be needed, as this was the only place he wanted to be. He loved the coil of smoke that he'd see rising from his house, like a beacon telling him to come home. The smile spread from his heart to his face, tugging his lips upward, crinkling his eyes.

A late-spring wind whipped around his hair, filling his nose with the last scents of melting snow, rubbing the branches together in a consistent song of twigs and the brown, scattered remnants of last year's leaves.

Two weeks had been long enough away. He never wanted to be gone for more than two weeks. But each trip away made their reunions so much sweeter.

The moment the horse stepped its foot in town, the sound fell away.

No.

The blood drained from his face. He whipped his head frantically behind him to ensure the wind was still moving. Yes, the branches continued to dance. Dried leaves were still blowing to and fro. His eyes shot to the tavern where a small pool of yellow light spilled out from the window. There would be music. There would be people.

He heard nothing.

The night had no sound. Not even a whisper.

He practically fell off his horse, tumbling to the ground, pumping his arms and begging his legs to carry him forward just like he were running up Uaimh Reev's sheerest mountain as he sprinted to his house.

Someone—or something—had a dampener. His heart thundered in his ears, adrenaline coursing through his veins. A dampener. Nothing good came from a dampener. His fingertips had filled with blood, feeling his pulse everywhere in his body as the high-pitched ringing of fear that only occurred between the ears became the only sound. Even his own feet made no noise against the grass.

No sound. There was no sound.

He rounded the corner and skidded to a halt, heart dropping into his stomach.

No. No, no, no.

He recognized the man immediately as he stopped, frozen to the ground. A slow smile spread across the merchant's face.

Odrin couldn't breathe.

"You did wait for me to see you, didn't you? After you took my reason for living? The only thing that brought me purpose? It seemed only sporting that I do the same."

Perhaps there was meant to be more, but Odrin didn't need to hear the rest.

He didn't wait for an explanation, monologues, lunges, attacks, or anything. The merchant had barely raised his pathetic sword in a startled defensive reaction before Odrin's blade cleaved his head clean from his shoulders. The moment the man's head hit the ground, the dampening fell away. The rolling sound of the head on grass joined the sudden onslaught of noise, from the rubbing of trees to the distant chatter of patrons in the tavern.

No.

This couldn't be happening.

This wasn't real.

He didn't stop to look at the fallen man, at the blood, at the headless merchant in the center of the village, but ran into the house, terror, sorrow, fear, and panic tearing through him.

His front door was ajar.

He tore into the room, eyes wild.

"Effie!" he screamed, falling to his knees. The wail that came from his belly was so unhinged, so untethered from the earthly plane that few could ever be said to have shared such a sound or such a sorrow as he scooped his hands through the pool of blood, clutching her lifeless body to him. He clenched her for the barest of moments before releasing her, searching for the wound.

Something clattered to the floor as the sound of a dagger freeing itself from her cold grip broke his lost sense of confusion. She'd tried fighting back, just like he'd shown her.

"Wait, Effie, wait!" he commanded, easing her back down

into her crimson puddle as he took off for the tonics he kept stored in their cabinet.

She could not listen. She could do no waiting. There was no one there to wait.

He returned with the tonic, opening her mouth and pouring in one vial, lifting her head to try to make her swallow. The liquid spilled out of her mouth, her eyes still unseeing.

"Effie, no, you have to swallow. Swallow, Effie! Listen to me!" he begged. He shook her, feeling himself poised to tumble from his place in the world into utter despair. He blinked suddenly, head whipping up from his wife. "Yrsa?" He rose to his feet and stopped before reaching the bassinet. He didn't have to get to the crib to see the red droplets of blood that had saturated the fabric, hitting the floor with slow, rhythmic consistency.

Yes.

It was real.

It was all real.

Odrin fell to the floor and let his sorrow pour out like a burst dam. Wave after wave of pain, of sobbing, of agony hit him, raking his body, unraveling him from his core and scattering him to the wind until there was nothing left. He couldn't breathe. He couldn't think. He couldn't exist.

His clothes wet with the cold blood of his dead wife, he buried his face in his hands and wept.

PART SIX
ANTLERS

He was silent and would be for a long, long time.

Today was not meant for voices.

Odrin took his careful time as he bathed them both, cleaning their hair, their bodies, their essence of any evidence of the atrocities that had been committed. He'd used her favorite soaps, the ones that smelled of apples and autumn. His eyes remained dry as moved her limp, blue-gray body, maneuvering her cold shape into her prettiest clothes. He dressed Effie in her favorite lilac dress, knowing she'd always felt like the goddess herself when she wore it. He chose a tiny, white gown for his perfect, innocent daughter. He combed Effie's hair but did not braid it. She would have wanted it unbound. Life had not granted Yrsa the time she needed to grow hair. He tucked her against her mother's arms, resting his tiny she-bear against the breast of his beloved. Against her heart in life and in death.

The two women, the only things in the world he cared about, slept with perfect stillness, eyes closed forever as they held each other.

Effie's father, along with the men from the village, was standing in quiet vigil outside the house. Odrin cradled his wife and daughter in his arms, carrying them with slow, careful dignity from the house to the top of the hill where he laid them to rest. Her parents had wanted to bury their daughter and grandchild in the cemetery behind the church, but Odrin had insisted that there was only one place she'd want to rest. He'd spent the morning digging their grave himself. The carpenter had met him on the hilltop with her cedar coffin, big enough for her to cradle their child into the afterlife.

Odrin didn't cry through the funeral, though her parents had been fractured shells, scarcely more than pieces of themselves. He couldn't speak, couldn't say any words in her eulogy. No one in the village blamed him. There had never been two people more in love. No one doubted his heart, his fidelity, or the well of his sorrow.

He was a man unmade.

They lowered Effie and Yrsa into the earth and covered the grave with fresh soil. The blacksmith had forged the symbol of the All Mother at Odrin's request to put as their tombstone, two parallel lines and one curved half circle about one third of the way down made from iron. Pretty words and prayers and blessings were said, and then it was over. Everyone would move on with their life. The villagers would forget about them. Grass would grow over their graves. The seasons would change. The world would go on.

His father-in-law patted him on the back, looking away with red eyes. Effie's mother hugged him, and the embrace cracked the pieces of her that remained, scattering her fragmented. heart to the wind once more as she sobbed. Odrin held his mother-in-law until she was strong enough to leave with her husband, knowing their hearts would never heal. Others had shaken his hand, and still more had given him the respect of space and privacy.

Then silence.

At last, he was on their hill alone.

The lightest mist of rain began to dampen the world, new earth mingling with the last bits of melting snow in the freshest scents of early spring. He took his time collecting a few of the small white and purple flowers that grew on the hillside, their tiny blossoms always the first sign of the early season, and laid them on her grave. He knelt on the soil near her head.

Odrin touched the antler against his chest, the one with the small letter e engraved by a teenage girl in an apple orchard who'd told him with pure conviction that she'd always be with him. He took the other necklace from his pocket and draped the matching counterpart around her iron headstone, a little antler with the letter o for her to wear in the afterlife.

"My heart will belong to no one else." His voice broke off in a sob as he clenched his eyes against the tears he hadn't shed during the eulogy. They flowed freely now, watering the white and purple flowers that had decorated his hair when he was a child pretending to be a boy deer with his favorite person. "I was supposed to be your guardian angel," he said with a choked voice, touching the iron and closing his eyes. "Now you'll have to be mine."

AFTERWORD

Remain in Gyrradin with completed *The Night and Its Moon* quartet and accompanying novellas. The villain duology, *A Chill in the Flame*, and *A Frozen Pyre* reveal the creation of the continent's demons, the origin of Uaimh Reev and the league of peacekeeping assassins, and the last fae royals of Farehold.

<u>Odrin's story pairs well with:</u>
Parting Glass Feat. Lauren Paley *by* The Wellermen
Whiskey Neat

CONTENT WARNINGS

themes of grief, loss, death of loved ones, infant death, alcohol, sexuality, mature language, on-page murder and violence.

THE DEER AND THE DRAGON

NO OTHER GODS

Read on for an excerpt of the urban mythology series

CHAPTER ONE

April 15, age 26

I STARED down the barrel of the lesser of two evils: the flesh-and-blood disappointment of a human man, or a life trapped in my imagination with a fictional lover.

I remembered reading that the brain stops forming at twenty-six. I watched the man across from me chew his food with his mouth slightly ajar, not bothering to swallow before he went on to name-drop yet another notch in society's belt. He was holding his chopsticks wrong. He had mixed wasabi directly into his soy sauce. He'd spoken at a cringe-worthy volume throughout the meal, drawing curious, if disgruntled, stares. There wasn't a single etiquette he followed, and it wasn't even close to the worst thing about him.

I wasn't sure if I hoped the bit about the brain was true. I was halfway through my twenty-sixth year and not so sure that this was the finished product I wanted for my mind. I was doing my best to be normal. This was what normal people did, right? They went on terrible dates with ordinary humans. They didn't see things that weren't there. They didn't cling to ghosts and maladaptive fantasies they'd conjured in the dark. They took their meditations, they went to therapy, and they learned how to distinguish what was real.

If my brain had stopped forming, however, it might come with perks. On the one hand, it meant that this bovine-mannered date wouldn't be a core memory. The man in the suit across from me—Jared? Joshua? I'm pretty sure it was Josh—would be a forgettable date after a long string of mediocre sex and dating apps. On the other hand, maybe it meant my courtship habits and hidden, wish-fulfilling coping mechanisms were cemented in stone and there was no hope for me. Perhaps I was doomed to repeat a cycle of Joshes. This was my curse.

"Marlow?"

Oh, fuck. He was staring at me. Had he asked me a question? I squinted my eyes slightly, peering through the din of the too-expensive restaurant and the polite chatter of upscale patrons for a clue.

"Come again?" I attempted an apologetic smile.

His perplexed look was one I understood. Of course he would be confused that I hadn't been listening. This was our second date, and he expected more from me. After all, I'd been utterly delightful last time. Painted, waxed, and squeezed into the most stunning dress, sporting the glossiest hair and the most charming smiles, I was a living superlative. I'd spent my life learning how to make the perfect first impression.

My profile had been curated to snag any curious suitor. First was a high-resolution picture that a friend had taken four years prior on a boat in Rio de Janeiro, where the greens and grays of the coast matched my eyes. "Where was that picture taken?" gave prospective dates an easy conversation opener. The next two had been selected to attract the outdoorsy types, from the HD pic of me flexing on a mountain in yoga pants and a sports bra to me on the beach laughing with friends—which also created the perfect excuse to show off a bikini body and gave me an easy way to screen out anyone who didn't like curves. I rounded out the profile with a picture of me alone with my coffee cup and computer, looking very serious and business-like, immediately followed by a photo of me jumping on the bed holding a bottle of wine, dress flying up, muddy blond curls a cloud around my face, smiling as if I were having the time of my life. Whatever dream you wanted to project onto me, I gave you the option right there in my intricately tailored series of images.

"Who are you?" the app had asked.

"Whoever you need me to be," my profile replied.

Every date was spent in a song and dance of asking the right questions, laughing at the right pitch, tossing my hair over my shoulder, arching my neck, lowering my lashes, and, as always, keeping them talking. They'd leave thinking they'd met their soulmate. I'd leave wondering if I could catch the newest episode of *Fire and Swords* or if I'd have to wait until it was on a streaming service.

"I asked if you've been to the Galápagos," he repeated.

"No." I kept my tone as light as possible. I glanced down at the elaborately plated omakase sushi that had doubtlessly cost more than half of the country made in a month. This was why I'd agreed to go on the second date. I loved good sushi, and free just so happened to be my favorite price. The salmon belly was the most well marbled in the hemisphere. I'd come back with terrible company just to eat my weight in the stuff even if it meant thinking about what sort of life these ocean animals had before they ended up on my plate.

He grabbed the sake kettle and tilted the alcohol into his glass first, then mine.

I kept the disarming smile on my face as I said, "I've wandered my way through a lot of South America, but I was teaching English as a second language and I—"

"Oh, you have to go back and do it the right way. I have a friend who works at the most incredible resort you've ever seen. The fish swim right underneath..." His mouth kept moving as my thoughts drifted into the restaurant's ambience while I started to think of marine life. I liked aquariums. I wondered how long it had been since I'd been to one. Maybe I'd go to the city's aquatic zoo, bring a bag of magic mushrooms, pop in my headphones, and listen to music while counting sharks over the weekend.

Josh required little encouragement to continue the conversation. It only took a pleading look to the waitress and a firm *"No,"* when asked if we wanted desserts for her to bring the check without waiting for his argument on digestifs. She knew from the very intentional way I'd selected designer pieces, from the delicate chain around my neck to the bag that dangled over the back of my chair, that I could afford the bill if I'd requested it. My deadpan stare challenged him to give it to me. In my early twenties, I would have rushed to cover the check so that Josh wouldn't expect anything from me. Now I expected him to procure his Amex as penance for making me watch him chew with his mouth open. It was the least he could do.

I idly wondered if Josh had ever asked me what I did for a living. Perhaps that was my own fault. I'd gotten so good at getting others to talk about themselves that I'd become excellent at living in the shadows. I wonder how many of my dates knew more about me than my name and how spectacular I was in bed.

We'd scarcely stepped into the cold, cloudless night before he asked, "So, should we go back to my place?"

"Oh." I pouted slightly to underscore my feigned regrets while shrugging into my coat, saying, "I'm so sorry. I called a rideshare while I was in the bathroom. It's only two minutes out."

Josh looked like he'd been slapped. I wondered how many times a man with a forty-thousand-dollar Rolex was turned down. Then again, it had been a running pleasure of mine to play catch and release. The bigger the fish, the more satisfying it was to throw them back into the water. Everything about this evening had me wishing I'd stayed in to watch the documentary about whales rather than wasting the perfume by stepping out into the world.

"What about the concert?"

I frowned, scarcely looking up from my phone. "Concert?"

Confusion faded into agitation as he studied my face. "Next week, the one I—"

Fish. Everything about this man was a fish. When they tell you that there are plenty of fish in the sea, they forget to mention that half of marine life is boring, scaly and a part of an identical school of thousands just like him. I would rather be alone, high, and looking at tropical fish next weekend. "Oh, I'm so sorry, Josh—this is my car!"

"It's Jacob."

I grimaced. I really was sorry about that one. I should have checked his name from the dating profile when I'd escaped to the restroom.

He knew the evening had soured but still had the balls to go in for a kiss. I intercepted with a side hug before launching into the street to stop my car. I closed the door and took off into the night before my date had time to recover from his wounded ego. The driver asked precisely the right number of questions, which was zero. He left me alone to the buzzing phone that illuminated the back seat of the vehicle.

(Kirby) How was the banker?
(Nia) CFO, right? Big money
(Kirby) Not like tech guy. Mar, could you call him up again?
We used to go to much nicer places when you were
sleazing it with the tech guy.
(Marlow) I'd like to sleaze it up with a loose bag of cheese
and my sweatpants
(Nia) You were supposed to get laid. How am I supposed

to live vicariously through you if you're pulling a celibacy
act
(Kirby) No, that's fair. She's always been a slut for cheese.
No one made you get married, Nia.
(Nia) And so what? I'm supposed to live with the conse-
quences of my actions?
(Marlow) I'm just going to call it an early night
(Nia) And waste a great hair and makeup day? Damn, there
must be some fantastic cheese back at your place

I clicked the button on the side of my phone, turning the
screen into an obsidian mirror and leaned my head against the
window, watching the black and auburn blur of homes, shadows, lawns, and fences as we crossed through a neighborhood.
I used to look at houses and wonder about the lives of the
people who lived inside. What did the family do to afford a
home so close to downtown? What did a three-story house
with fantastic landscaping cost in one of the world's flashiest
cities? It had been a long time since I'd cared.

I saw the driver frown as the GPS turned into the northern
part of the metropolis. It wasn't an unusual reaction. No one
lived in the warehouse district. There was no reason for a girl
of any repute to take a car to the warehouses in high heels and
red lipstick. He pulled up along the sidewalk and eyed what
had once been a bread factory. His expression deepened into
worry at the smattering of lights and darkened entryway.

"Is this right, miss?"

"Home sweet home." I smiled. I flashed him my screen to
show the glowing rating I'd sent his way as I slid out of the car.
His eyebrows remained knit, but he shrugged as I closed the
door. He wasn't paid enough to care.

A blanket-like quiet pressed in as the car pulled away—a
sound challenging to achieve anywhere in the city. There was
no traffic, no pedestrians, no indication that anyone but the
phantoms of long-dead industry tycoons haunted these corri-

dors. The April night clung to the last of spring's chill, sending goose bumps up and down my bare legs. I fished a metallic rose-gold card from my purse and pressed it against the panel, satisfied when it buzzed.

I rounded the brick corridor for the atrium, where an ever-attentive receptionist waited to respectfully greet me. She was one of four and arguably my favorite. No matter how short my skirt, how high my heels, or how late the hour, she remained polite without speaking. I knew her boyfriend's name, I gave her chocolates every holiday, and we never failed to gush about the new episodes of *Fires and Swords* if I loitered in the hallway, but she had an innate gift for knowing when I was overwhelmed and needed silence. Perhaps intuition was a prerequisite for anyone who took a job in luxury apartments.

Though she'd never say it outright, her expressions conveyed the same long-standing concern that I'd stumbled through the door after too many dates to count. She'd helped me get into the building when I was a bit too drunk to see my phone and buzzed me up to my room whenever I'd lost too much brain function to recall how my card worked. It seemed like a safe bet that she was not the sort of person who got high at aquariums.

The small bank of polished elevators waited quietly, all in disuse given the lateness of the hour. One opened for me the moment I pressed the button.

I didn't wait for the elevator doors to close before slipping out of my heels, dangling the sharpened ends from one hand. I caught the brief, disapproving narrowing of eyes through the rapidly closing doors and flashed my most dazzling smile. Part of me respected her bravery. It was bold to be judgmental of the residents when they knew precisely how much these apartments cost.

I pressed the glittery, metallic card onto the pad to gain access to my floor—second from the top. The penthouse hadn't been available, and I'd been okay with it. Everyone who lived here had their reasons for wanting to stay off the world's radar, and there wasn't a better establishment in the city for those with deep enough pockets to erase themselves from the map. The building's discretion had been worth the downgrade, and as someone who lived alone, I couldn't have justified the extra space unless I was looking to install a private bowling alley.

The elevator door opened noiselessly onto my floor. There were thirteen units in the entire building—two per floor, save for the lucky bastard who'd snagged the thirteenth. I walked barefoot down the sparkling black marble to my room and pressed my thumb into the pad, allowing it to scan my fingerprint until a subtle click told me the mechanisms had unlocked.

It was dark in my apartment and stayed that way. I'd had the features for automatic lights disabled the day I'd moved in.

I tossed my purse onto the floor, leaving it in a jumble with my shoes. I walked to the window and stared out over the twinkling lights of the city and the sliver of river I could spot from my unit. I was a sucker for a good view.

The hairs on the back of my neck prickled in the way they did when one knew they were being watched. The rush of gin, moss, and mist filled the room the moment before I heard it. I breathed it in like a prayer.

"Leave it open" came a male voice from the shadows.

I fought the deep, conflicting bloom that emanated from somewhere near my center. My toes curled, heart thundering at the purr of his voice. "Don't do this to me," I grumbled halfheartedly, but I was certain he heard the ghost of a smile in my voice.

"Didn't go well?" he asked.

I continued facing the window but reached over my head for the zipper. Years had gone by, and I was still breathless every time he spoke. It was so easy to lose my resolve whenever those silken words tumbled over his lips. I managed to give the thin metal a tug but lost my grip on it as I said, "He was utterly forgettable."

"They all will be," he said, brushing my hair away from my neck. Goose bumps started at the nape of my neck and slithered down my spine. He held the top of my dress in one strong hand, using the other to gently tug the zipper. He stopped before releasing it more than a quarter of an inch. I waited for the next sensation, but nothing came. Tension swelled as I swallowed another deep breath of earth and perfume.

"What?" I breathed.

The electric current of his touch coursed through me.

"Holy fuck," I murmured, falling to pieces.

His fingers began to work their way up the hem of my dress, nudging it up over my hips. My stomach clenched. My lips parted in a stifled gasp, eyes closing as he came up behind me. His mouth sucked gently on the tender place where my throat met my shoulder. Every sense in my body homed in on the delicious sensation. His mouth moved to the back of my neck, hands dropping from my hips to urge me forward. I leaned into the floor-to-ceiling glass, letting the cold seep into me as his hand slid from my inner thigh, higher, *higher.*

"Oh god," I gasped when he grazed the soaked evidence of my black-lace panties.

"You know better than that," he chided softly at my choice in words, a teasing warmth in his voice. He relaxed his body into mine until I was pressed wholly against the window. "Now, are you going to let me in?"

My face betrayed the battle going on in my head and heart. My body ached for him. My breasts peaked against the thin dress. The pulsing in my chest extended into every piece of me, and I felt my heartbeat in my greediest places. My fingers clenched against the glass. He chuckled lightly.

"Nothing without your permission," he said, fingers still grazing me with tantalizing slowness. The tingle of the water between my legs trickling onto my inner thighs elicited a low groan of approval. His fingers continued to move over the thin fabric.

I gasped against the sensation, and he leaned into my throat once more, smiling through my pleasure.

"You know I'm..." Words felt useless.

"You're what?" he pressed me into the window with more force.

"I'm trying to stop."

His fingers quickened as he said, "As if I don't know you, Love. We both know it'll never make you happy. But if you'd prefer mundane restaurants and forgettable men over what I can offer you..." His hand stilled.

My lust, my greed, my denial came out in a single, short sound. My eyes opened as I turned back to the shadows, but I knew what I'd see before I turned.

Despite the bandage-tight dress around my hips and the puddle of evidence on my legs, I knew he wasn't there. He hadn't been there in a long, long time.

THE DEER AND THE DRAGON
NO OTHER GODS

This new series from Piper CJ is the start of an urban fantasy based on the real world. As war looms, it's a fight for survival, a pantheon of deities and a belief in love, all working together to build an epic narrative.

"HOW DOES A HUMAN GIRL LOSE THE PRINCE OF HELL?"

Marlow needs to believe she's crazy. The alternative would mean embracing the gift—or curse—shared by her mother and grandmother: she can see angels and demons, including a dark and haunting entity who's been with Marlow her entire life. At least, she believes that's all he is until a fae from the Nordic pantheon strolls into her life and informs her that she's been sharing a bed with the Prince of Hell.

A Prince who's now gone *missing*.

Before she knows it, Marlow is deeply entangled in a centuries-old war, stumbling straight into a battleground between mighty beings of myth and legend from powerful pantheons around the world. And who will come out on top may just depend on her and the love she never dared to believe in.

FOR FANS OF:
- Romantasy
- Mythology & folklore
- Kickbutt heroines
- Fae, angels, and demons
- Hilarious banter
- *Hazbin Hotel*

ABOUT THE AUTHOR

Piper CJ, author of the USA Today bisexual fantasy series *The Night and Its Moon,* urban mythology series *No Other Gods,* and New York Times bestselling series *Fern's School for Wayward Fae,* is a photographer, hobby linguist, and French fry enthusiast. She has an M.A. in Folklore and a B.A. in Broadcasting, which she used in her former life as a morning-show weather girl, hockey podcaster, and in audio documentary work. Now when she isn't playing with her dog, she's gaming, binging cartoons, dissecting fairy tales, or disappointing her parents.

website: pipercj.com

instagram.com/piper_cj
tiktok.com/pipercj

www.ingramcontent.com/pod-product-compliance
Lightning Source LLC
Chambersburg PA
CBHW060339310726

48976CB00007B/2621